Tilbury House Publishers • 12 Starr Street, Thomaston, Maine 04861 • 800-582-1899 • www.tilburyhouse.com

Text and illustrations © 2017 by Michael Garland

Hardcover ISBN 978-088448-588-9 • eBook ISBN 978-9-88448-590-2
First hardcover printing September 2017 • 15 16 17 18 19 20 XXX 10 9 8 7 6 5 4 3 2 1

Library of Congress Control Number: 2017937851

Cover and interior designed by Frame25 Productions • Printed in Korea through Four Colour Print Group, Louisville, KY
April 2017 • Printed by WeSP Corp. Ltd, Gyeonggi-do, South Korea • 79107

This book is dedicated to
Muddy Waters, Willie Dixon, John Lee Hooker,
Lightning Hopkins, and B.B. King.

DADDY PLAYED THE BLUES

MICHAEL GARLAND

TILBURY HOUSE PUBLISHERS, THOMASTON, MAINE

I was six years old in 1936 the day we left the farm in Mississippi.
Between the boll weevils, the floods, and the landlord, there was no
way a family could scratch out a living there anymore.

Mama cried into her handkerchief and said,

"Okay Cassie. Get in the car. It's time to go."

Daddy told us, "There are jobs up north in Chicago. So that's where we're going."

Mama, Daddy, my brothers James and Aaron, Uncle Vernon, and I all squeezed into our old car. Everything we owned was squished in the trunk or tied on the roof.

I sat in the backseat with the boys. Across our laps was Daddy's most prized possession, a six-string guitar in a beat-up case.

As we drove along, I thought about Daddy and Uncle Vernon and how they always liked to sit on the porch after a long workday and play the blues.

Mama said she didn't like the blues because it wasn't church music, but after a while, I would always see her tapping her foot to the music.

It took two or three days to drive from Fayette, Mississippi to Chicago, Illinois. We were at the very beginning when Daddy started to hum a tune as he drove. Uncle Vernon took out his harmonica and played softly.

Mama sat between them trying to disapprove, but a little smile kept appearing at the corners of her mouth.

I don't remember where we slept or what we ate. But I remember one of the blues songs Daddy sang as the car snaked along the winding road.

Goin' down this road and I'm feelin' bad, baby,
Goin' down this road feelin' so miserable and bad,
I ain't gonna be treated this way.

Blues songs are about sad things like broken hearts and being far from home and about hard things like working long hours and being poor.

No matter how sad the song, Daddy always said it made him feel better to sing it. It sure made me feel better to hear it.

When we finally arrived in Chicago, we stayed with our cousins until
Daddy and Uncle Vernon found work in the stockyards.
Then we rented a little apartment on the South Side.

Even though we were in a new place, *some* things never change.
As soon as Daddy and Uncle Vernon got home from work, they
would sit right down on the front stoop and start playing.

In no time at all they found other musicians to play with. If Daddy and Uncle Vernon weren't *playing* the blues, they were *talking* about the blues. They would go on late into the evening talking about WC Handy and Blind Lemon Jefferson or a woman named Bessie Smith.

My favorite song was the "Catfish Blues." When Daddy played
it, Mama would laugh and shake her head.

What if I were a catfish, mama?
I said, swimmin' deep down in, deep blue sea.
Have these gals now, sweet mama, settin' out,
Settin' out hooks for me, for me, settin' out hooks for, for me.

Sometimes when Daddy sang the song called "The Little
Red Rooster," it made me homesick for the farm.

Dogs begin to bark now
And the hounds begin to howl,
Dogs begin to bark now
And the hounds begin to howl,
Watch out stray cat,
The little red rooster's on the prowl.

I wanted to stay up and listen, but Mama always sent me to bed. Sometimes on a night like this, I would fall asleep with the sound of the music in my ears, dreaming about Robert Johnson waiting at the crossroads for the devil to come.

I went down to the crossroad
fell down on my knees,
I went down to the crossroad
fell down on my knees . . .

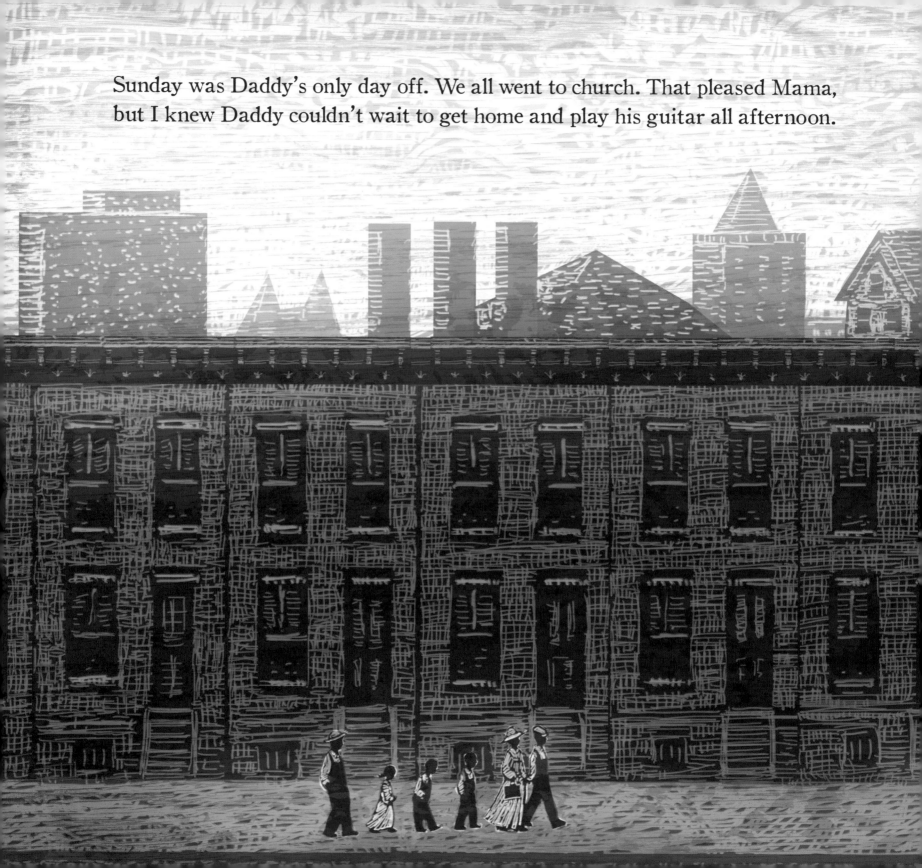

Sunday was Daddy's only day off. We all went to church. That pleased Mama, but I knew Daddy couldn't wait to get home and play his guitar all afternoon.

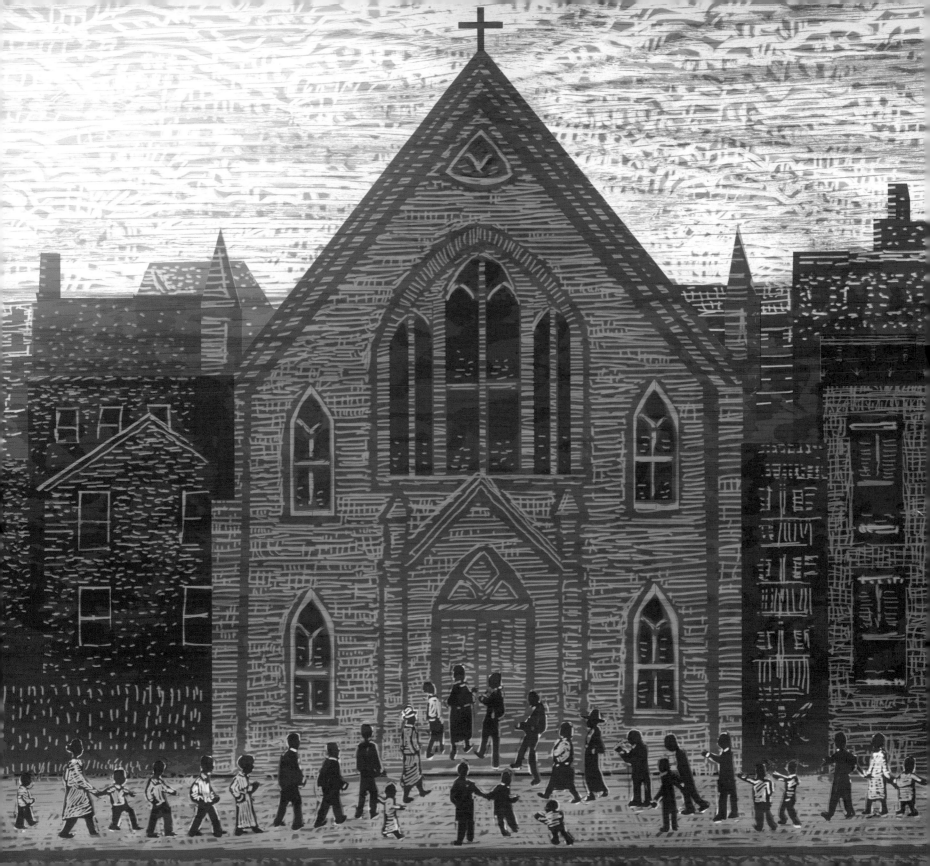

Those Sundays were so long ago, but I can still see my daddy strumming and singing with Uncle Vernon and their friends in our little front room.

Mama would look at Daddy and laugh, "Now, there is one happy man."

Author's Note

I first became interested in popular music as a child. Among my favorites were the Rolling Stones, the Animals, the Cream, and Van Morrison. Without knowing it, I was introduced to the blues.

Mick Jagger and Keith Richards began their friendship as young boys in Dartford, England, when Keith showed Mick a schoolbag full of blues records. It was the beginning of the Rolling Stones, a name taken from the Muddy Waters song "Rollin' Stone."

As I came to know more about music, I learned that songs like "Love in Vain" and "Cross Roads" were not original compositions by the Rolling Stones and Cream, but had been written long before by American bluesmen Muddy Waters and Robert Johnson. When I finally had an opportunity to hear the original versions of these songs, I realized how much better and more authentic they sounded.

It is funny to think that the uniquely American art form of blues music had to be reflected back to America from across the Atlantic Ocean before many Americans had an opportunity to hear it. Once I was old enough to go to concerts, I was able to attend a blues show at Carnegie Hall in New York with two legendary headliners, Muddy Waters and Willie Dixon.

In the years since, I've attended many blues concerts, mostly in small venues. I've heard artists like John Lee Hooker, Lightning Hopkins, and B.B. King—three all-time greats—performing in the twilights of their careers.

Blues music evolved in the southern United States when African Americans fused African traditional music with spirituals, work songs, and European and American folk ballads. After that, blues music followed the Great Migration north as many poor African Americans fled the oppressive agrarian economy of the South in search of opportunities and employment. These seekers were former slaves or descendants of slaves who were trapped in the sharecropper system, in which tenant farmers paid rent or a portion of their crops to landowners.

Families like Cassie's barely got by even in the good years. Jobs in the North paid more and offered relief from the Jim Crow laws of the South, which denied African Americans the right to vote and segregated blacks from whites.

The Great Migration lasted from about 1910 until 1970, with a pause during the years of World War II. Although Cassie and her family are fictional characters, great multitudes of real people made the trip from Mississippi to Chicago, Illinois. Others fled Alabama, Louisiana, Texas, and Georgia for cities like New York, Philadelphia, Pittsburgh, and Detroit. Still others journeyed west to Los Angeles, San Francisco, Seattle, and Portland.

Chicago blues was a new style of music born from this migration. McKinley Morganfield, later known as Muddy Waters, made the trip from Rolling Fork, Mississippi to Chicago. Many people consider him to be "the Father of Chicago Blues."

Keith Richards told a story about the Rolling Stones' first visit to a sacred place in blues mythology, Chicago's Chess Records. When they walked through the door, the first person they met was Muddy Waters. Muddy was down on his luck, so the owners of Chess Records had hired him to paint the office. The Stones were young millionaires, and Muddy was still grinding hard to put food on the table. It seems sad and unfair, but the bright side was that the Stones and other blues-inspired rock-and-roll bands turned a whole new generation on to the blues. Many of the great bluesmen enjoyed a revitalization of their careers in a brand-new spotlight.

Whenever I hear a good blues song, I think of the people and places that inspired the music and lyrics. Those songs were my inspiration for writing *Daddy Played the Blues*.

Michael Garland

Song Credits

"Goin' Down the Road Feelin' Bad" is an American traditional song with an unknown author. This song was first recorded by Henry Whitter as the "Lonesome Road Blues" in 1924. It was later recorded by Big Bill Broonzy, Woody Guthrie, Bill Monroe, Earl Scruggs, and the Grateful Dead.

"Catfish Blues" was written by Robert Petway in 1941 and was one of only sixteen songs Petway recorded in his life. "Catfish Blues" was later recorded by Muddy Waters, John Lee Hooker, and Jimi Hendrix.

"Little Red Rooster" is credited to Willie Dixon, but it may be based on earlier songs by Charlie Patton, Howlin' Wolf, and Memphis Minnie. Sam Cook and the Rolling Stones recorded their own versions.

"Cross Road Blues" was written by Robert Johnson in 1936. Elmore James and Eric Clapton with the Cream reinterpreted Johnson's song.

Jimi Hendrix

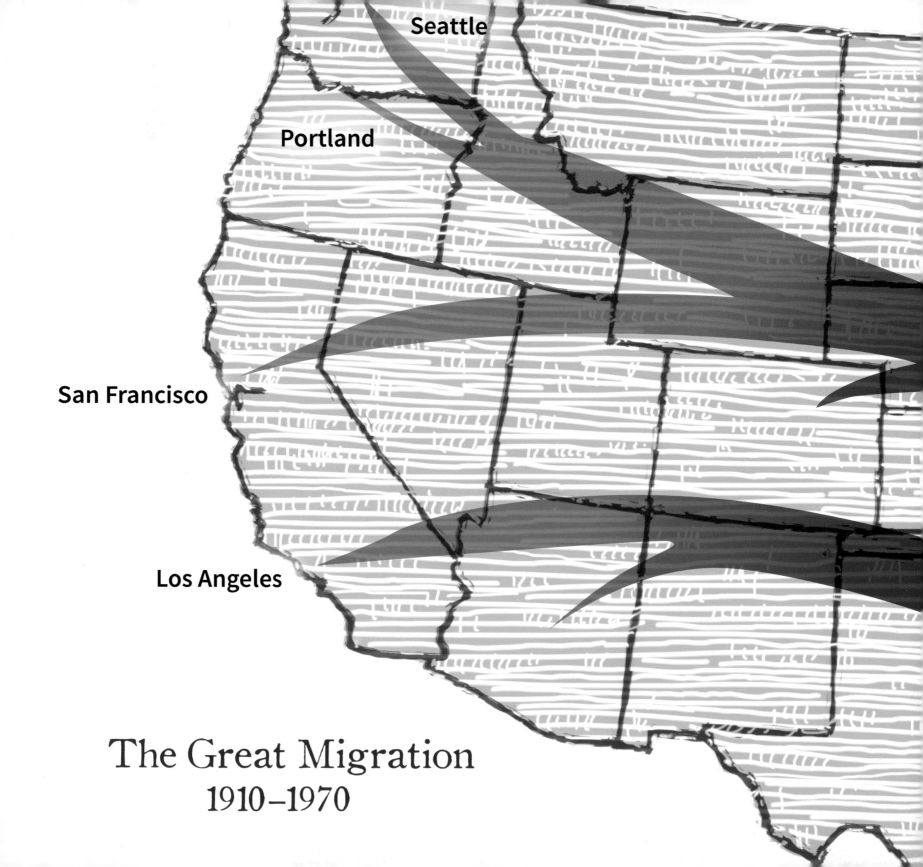

Seattle

Portland

San Francisco

Los Angeles

The Great Migration
1910–1970

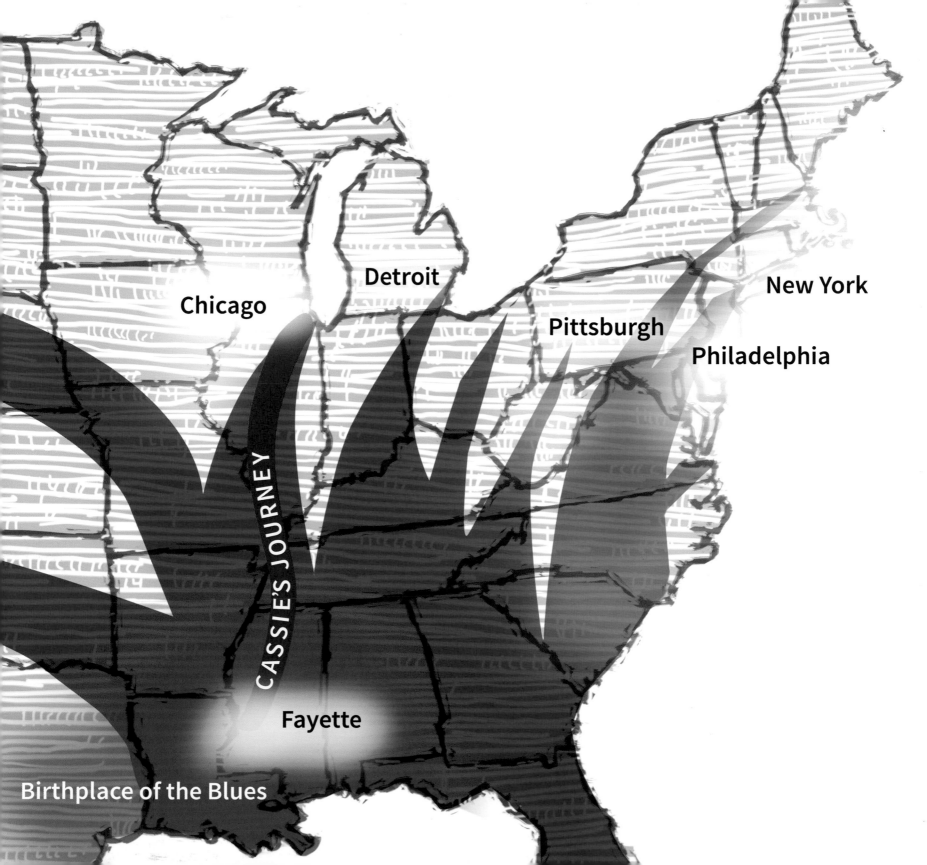

Chicago

Detroit

New York

Pittsburgh

Philadelphia

CASSIE'S JOURNEY

Fayette

Birthplace of the Blues

ROBERT JOHNSON (May 8, 1911–August 16, 1938) had a short career and life, dying at age twenty-seven. Born in Hazelhurst, Mississippi, he gained little fame in his lifetime but is now considered a master of the Mississippi Delta style of blues. When a collection of his music was reissued in 1961, a new generation of fans celebrated his music, and his fame became widespread.

BESSIE SMITH (April 15, 1894–September 26, 1937) was the most popular female blues singer from 1920 to 1930, in the Roaring Twenties. Born in Chattanooga, Tennessee, Bessie became the highest-paid black entertainer of her time. She was known as the Empress of the Blues.

MUDDY WATERS (April 4, 1913–April 30, 1983) was McKinley Morganfield's professional stage name. He was born in Rolling Fork, Mississippi, but migrated to Chicago when he was thirty to become a professional bluesman. He is known as the Father of Chicago Blues.

WILLIE DIXON (July 1, 1915–January 29, 1992), born in Vicksburg, Mississippi, is the writer of many great blues songs. Although he played guitar, he is more famous for his upright bass. Willie stands alongside Muddy Waters as a pioneer of the Chicago blues sound.

JOHN LEE HOOKER (August 22, 1912–June 21, 2001) was born the son of a sharecropper and Baptist preacher in Tutwiler or Clarksdale, Mississippi. Taught to play the guitar by his stepfather, John Lee became famous for his electrified style of delta blues.

LIGHTNING HOPKINS (March 15, 1911–January 30, 1982) was born in Centerville, Texas. He was inspired to become a bluesman after meeting Blind Lemon Jefferson at a church picnic when he was eight years old, and is considered a country blues musician.

BIG MAMA THORNTON (December 11, 1926–July 25, 1984) was born in Ariton or Montgomery, Alabama. A rhythm and blues singer and writer, her first number one record was "Hound Dog," the song that Elvis Presley later recorded and brought to an even larger audience.

HOWLIN' WOLF (June 10, 1910–January 10, 1976) was born in White Station, Mississippi. His real name was Chester Arthur (after the U.S. president). He too made the trip from Mississippi to Chicago, and one of his early producers was Sam Phillips, who later recorded Elvis for the first time.

WC HANDY (November 16, 1873–March 28, 1958) was born in Florence, Alabama. He brought the blues form to a much larger audience and is considered the Father of the Blues.

BLIND LEMON JEFFERSON (September 24, 1893–December 19, 1929) was born in Freestone County, Texas. Blind from birth, his real name was Lemon Henry Jefferson. He is sometimes called the Father of Texas Blues.

B.B. KING (September 16, 1925–May 14, 2015) was born on a cotton plantation near Itta Bena, Mississippi. The son of sharecroppers, B.B. earned the nickname the King of the Blues, and his guitar Lucille became one of the world's most famous musical instruments.

MICHAEL GARLAND is the author and illustrator of 34 children's picture books and the illustrator of more than 40 books written by others. *Miss Smith and the Haunted Library* is a *New York Times* bestseller. Other recent books include *Lost Dog, Tugboat, Car Goes Far, Fish Had a Wish* (starred review from *Publisher's Weekly*), *Where's My Homework?*, and *Grandpa's Tractor* (selected for the Original Art of Children's Book Show by the Society of Illustrators in NYC). Michael's *Christmas Magic* has become a seasonal classic. Michael created the illustrations for *Daddy Played the Blues* using a digital woodcut technique that he has pioneered.